VIDEOS

By Steven Bazydlo

Videos

Videos, Volume 1

Steven Bazydlo

Published by Steven Bazydlo, 2022.

Copyright/Trademark

This is a work of fiction. Similarities to real people, places, or events are entirely coincidental.

VIDEOS

First edition. March 16, 2022.

Copyright © 2022 Steven Bazydlo.

ISBN: 979-8215094822

Written by Steven Bazydlo.

Table of Contents

A mysterious box 1

Video: A walk in the woods 19

Video: Watching you sleep 27

Video: Crawlspace..39

Video: Shadows 49

Video: Daddy issues 59

Video: Friends 69

Lemseh Carothers-Abdullah- book jacket

Scott Dyson- Editor

Thank you to everyone who has helped me with this project.

A mysterious box

With the recent growth of social media and the many internet stars, it didn't take long for people to try to copy those who were successful in order to try and "get that bread." I hated the terms the internet has made popular. However, my best friend has fully embraced them and has become a stereotypical internet streamer in order to "get his slice," as he would put it.

"Hey bro, what's the plan fo dis weekend?"

"I don't know, maybe go to see a movie or go to the mall."

"Man, dat seems like some boring-ass bull shit. Maybe we can get some hot shorties and yeet some bread on dem bitches! I mean, Yolo, my brotha, let's do something fun."

I stared at him in silent awe because I didn't understand a fucking thing that he had just said. "Dude... What?"

"Bitch, what do you mean, what? I think I said it pretty crystal, ya hear?"

"Well..." Did I want a day of listening to Jimmy talk this way? No, but... "There's a place I found online I want to go check out."

"Word? Any hotties dere?"

"Um, no, but it might be a good video spot for your channel. I mean, you're all about trends, and isn't a major trend right now urban exploring?"

"Come on, bro. I'm trying to get my dangalang wetter than an otter."

"What the hell does that even mean? You know what, I don't want to know, but you asked what I was doing, and I told you. So you can join me or go try and find some ratchet chick to catch a disease from."

"Man, that shit sounds boring as hell, and don't talk about Veronica like dat. She got a cream to take care of da itchy twitchy down dere."

"Well, you could record the whole adventure and call it a ghost hunt or something. That might get you some views, and you know what more views means, right?"

"Oh, shit yeah, bitches love ghost shit!"

I honestly didn't know why I wanted him to come with me, but I knew I didn't want to be alone where we were going.

"So where dis place at?"

"I'll tell you in the morning. I'll bring everything we will need."

"How early? I mean, bro, I gots to get dem Z's."

"We can meet up at the old rail station at say ten o'clock?"

"Shit, dat's early on a Sunday, but okay. Dis place betta be worth it doe."

"If what I've researched is true, then it should be."

That night my excitement made it hard to sleep. I kept on imagining all the cool stuff we would find. This asylum had been abandoned since the inmates revolted and ended up burning half the building down. The other half was still intact, but it's been sitting in the woods for close to a hundred years. I couldn't wait to see what the local foliage had done to it.

I hope it wasn't like the last place I explored. Some of the more hooligan types had vandalized that property, breaking all the furniture and fixtures that remained and spray-painting all over the walls. The place had been a mess.

Who knows, maybe I'll find a cool souvenir or something today.

I spent the early morning hours gathering the few supplies we would need for our trip, and I felt a strange unease, like maybe we shouldn't be going, but that feeling passed when I got a message from Jimmy.

"Yo, this rise and shine bull shittery is wack as hell, boi. Oh, befo I foget. When the cameras be rollin, call me by my channel name, Bigtippy."

"Oh, for Christ's sake," I said, putting my face into my hands and sliding them down in minor annoyance and looking up at the ceiling before responding.

"Yep, no prob man. Remember. Old train station," I typed back to him.

"Yeah, yeah, already on my way."

Looking at the clock on my phone, I figured I should head out myself. I had spent far too long gathering some snacks and flashlights, but it was a long hike ahead of us.

Skipping down the stairs, I saw my stepdad sitting in the living room. His usual scowl plastered on his face, his attention focused on whatever sports page he'd found online while ignoring my mom, who seemed to be giving him the silent treatment while doing the dishes. They didn't ever seem to notice if I was home or not, even on a good day.

"Hey, you little shit, don't be out too late. It's a school night."

I stopped dead in my tracks. It was way out of his character to even acknowledge me. Let alone care if I was in class.

I glanced over to the kitchen and saw my mother already had a half-empty bottle of wine next to the sink and didn't seem to care that her husband was being a prick.

"Yeah, Rob, I hear ya."

His scowl seemed to deepen when I called him by his name. He hated the fact I refused to call him my father. But it's not like he was anything to measure up to my real dad.

The thought of my real dad filled me with sadness. I'll always miss him.

I took off out the door and headed towards the station. Just thinking of where my dad might be after he went out and never came back felt like a gut punch that I didn't wanna deal with right now.

The tracks were overgrown with weeds, and the dilapidated building was barely holding itself up, but what would you expect from a building as old as the town. I knew Jimmy, sorry "Bigtippy," would be here soon, but I still felt butterflies in my stomach.

I sat with my legs dangling off the edge of the platform next to the old terminal. The woods, even though it was early morning, were darkened by the thick leaves of the canopy above. The wind made them rustle and flail wildly as the trunks slowly swayed.

Feeling the breeze, I was filled with hope that today's adventure would be a great escape from the hell that awaited me back at home.

Closing my eyes, I listened to the sounds of nature as they sang their song of life. It was so calming that I almost forgot that I was still waiting on that ass-hat to get here. I don't know what was taking him so long. He lived closer than I did, yet I still managed to beat him here.

"This mother fucker better not have stoo–"

Just before I could finish my thought, I felt my legs pulled from beneath the platform. I fell to the ground and twisted, landing on my side but still knocking the wind out of me.

"Oi bitch boy, what you waitin fo, let's get this party started. I got a hot piece waiting for me when we get done, so let's go!"

"I've been waiting here for your dumb ass! What the hell was that for? You could have hurt me!"

"Oh, my bad, did I hurt you? Do you need a band-aid or me to kiss the boo-boo all better? Get up, you promised me a good video, and we gonna get dat bread today, boy!"

Turning away from me, he pulled out a camera and started shooting his introduction.

"Ehhhh, there my fine ass pimps and pimpettes, it's ya boy Bigtippy, and we have a hell of a show for you today. Let me introduce my bro here, who has the scoop on today's urban exploration. So, Squeaky, what's the low-down on this place we be going to?"

"First off, don't call me 'Squeaky.' Second, we are going to the abandoned Venerable Youth Asylum."

"Oh shit! We be going to where the cray-cray play, boys and girls. This should be fun. Hey, Squeaky, any chance we could find some ghosty-goos?"

I stared at him, a not-so-small part of me regretting having invited him. However, if he wasn't here and I got hurt... I would need him to get help.

"You and I both know those don't exist."

"Just cause we haven't seen dem don't mean they don't. Who knows, maybe we might catch some haunted shit without seeing it."

The pleading look on his face begging me to play along was sad, but I wasn't heartless. Figured I would humor him and maybe get us going.

"Sure, who knows, maybe a demon or something will jump out and smack you. We could run into a group of homeless people, or maybe just maybe we could get lucky, and some cult will be summoning their deranged deity of scat porn."

"Dat would be a sticky situation."

I felt a piece of me die inside as the words left my mouth, and I saw the glow in his eye.

He continued with his introduction, and I started to walk away. The excitement of the adventure ahead numbed the ache of hatred that the sound of his voice was stirring within me.

I heard him wrap up his segment. I didn't look back as the sound of his footsteps caught up to me, the railroad ties dampening the sound to a light patter.

"Yo, my boi! Hold up."

His voice was gasping for breath by the time he caught up.

"Wait, Squeaky! How far we be walkin fo dis?"

"We should be there in about forty-five minutes or so. It's only like four miles or so up the tracks." I shot daggers at him with my glare. "Call me 'Squeaky' again and I'm gonna lose you out here."

"Four miles!" he said with a little hesitation, ignoring my threat. "Man, there ain't nothin but fucking forest that way. Why da fuck would they even put a crazy hospital all da way out here anyways."

"They built it out here to keep the patients and the town safe. They used to hold the criminally insane there as well as some violent criminals."

"Really? Dat shit's dope as fuck. Why didn't you say dat when we was doin the intro, bro?"

Stopping for a second, I turned to Jimmy and looked him over.

"I didn't say that because why make this place a hot spot for people? What if we find something cool? Do you really want others showing up on your 'turf?'"

I could see the inner workings going on in his head like a hamster wheel spinning, but the hamster was dead before a smile creased his face.

"Boi, I like da way you think. Ya gotta keep dem otha fools out yo territory till we make our stacks."

The pep in his step seemed to be a little more consistent, if not faster now. We spent the time on the tracks mostly in silence until Bigtippy got bored and tried to rap to pass the time. It may have helped him, but it made time slow down to a crawl for me.

Finally, after his twenty-minute concert, I could see the platform for the hospital stop.

"And all deez bitches be..."

"Hey, shush! We're here."

"Oh, fo sho." Taking out his camera, he started filming again.

"Okay, so we here at the cray-cray play pen and dis shit about to be poppin. My boy here got us da low down on dis bitch. Apparently, dis place was housing some bad motha fuckas. Like for real for real."

His voice blurred into the distance as I continued down the tracks. The size of the building became more and more intimidating as the roof came into view through the branches. I knew from my research that the facility had five floors, three above ground and two below. It stretched the length of a small football field. The tree canopy waved in the wind, casting vaguely human-like shadows behind the pillars.

Hefting myself onto the concrete slab of the platform, I could better see that the building was in surprisingly good shape.

Not too much in the way of graffiti and most of the windows were still intact, regardless of the back of the building having been on fire.

I felt so mesmerized. My thoughts fixed on the odd shadows until one caught my eye. It wasn't moving like the others. It was unmoving against the shifting backdrop. It was a black, almost smoky hand.

I rubbed my eyes, and it was gone. *My brain must be screwing with me,* I thought, but it didn't change the small feeling of dread creeping into my stomach.

"Yo McSqueakums!" Jimmy snapped me out of my trance when he shoved me, making me stagger.

"Hey, what the hell, man?"

"Well, we gonna just stand out here lookin at it like some dime piece, or we gonna get in dare like we some big balla?"

"Oh, yeah, right. Um, let's go." I couldn't help but stammer. I looked back to the pillar, trying to figure out what I had seen, but my eyes must have been playing tricks because now I just saw the shadow of a branch.

Jimmy slapped my shoulder, and we stepped up to the main entrance. A set of large solid wood doors with ornate metal fixtures greeted us. The handle and lock were missing; a small hole in the wood showed their former location. We looked at each other, and I felt my heart beating as we placed our hands on the old faded door and pushed. The doors moved.

We pushed open the ornate doors and saw that they led into a three-story atrium. The welcome desk was the first thing we saw. The room was huge; the upper floors' balconies had railings and metal mesh enclosing the room.

"Dude, what's wit da chicken wire?"

"I think it was to prevent suicide attempts. I mean, that's a good thirty or forty feet straight down to the floor here."

"God damn, that would be such a savage way to go out. Like shit, on yo cause of death, it would say somethin cool like 'Squeaky head launched out ass into trash can for a three-pointer. May he rest in pieces.'"

I shuddered at the thought of how it would feel dying that way as he laughed out loud, causing an echo.

Looking around at the area, I noted that the years had been relatively kind to the asylum's interior. Some minor paint peeling and a few holes and liquor bottles, maybe from some rowdy kids, but still—it was in good shape nonetheless for being vacant for so long.

I walked around the reception desk and leaned against the counter. I don't know why, but I had this feeling that we were being watched. Not wanting to seem too scared, I occupied myself by searching the desk, where I found a map that clearly labeled where everything was. The top floor was marked as maximum security, the second floor was minimum, and the first floor was labeled as office space and labs. Searching a little more, I found another laminated map with what I assumed were the basement levels. A red smeared circle was around a room labeled "records room."

There we are. I wanna see what kind of people lived here, or what kind of history went on here, I thought.

"Hey, Jim...I mean, Bigtippy? Let's go down one of these hallways. Maybe we can find something cool."

Turning to his camera, Jimmy raised it to a cringe-worthy angle. "You hear dat boys and girls? We about to keep dis bitch movin and scootchy on down da way. Maybe we might catch some freaky bitch ass ghost."

I took another deep breath. *He swears so much during his videos that I'm surprised he can get monetized at all.* I looked down the unusually dark hallway to the left of us and felt my stomach turn. Not sure if it was out of excitement or fear, but either way, we were already here.

"This way," I said, gesturing down a hall that, according to the map I was carrying, should lead us to a stairwell.

The sound of the crunching leaves beneath my feet echoed in the near-silent hall. They must have been blown in over the years. We clearly weren't the first to explore here, and we still didn't know if we were alone either.

Our footsteps and Jimmy's babble resonated significantly louder in the smaller passageway. Surprisingly, the windows were still in good shape with only a few cracks and the occasional broken-out pane. The water damage that seeped through those holes discolored and warped the walls, clearly rotting away the slight padding that lined the walls.

We kept running into blocked hallways and locked doors, but after exploring the first floor for maybe an hour or so, we found a set of doors that stood out. Both had rusty red paint that had peeled off over time. The one sign to the left said, "2nd Floor," while the other said, "Basement."

"Looks like we have a fork in the road." I stood for a minute, trying to make a decision. Until I felt Jimmy grab my shoulder.

"Yo squeaky boy, imma head upstairs and get some B-roll shots for my followers. Where you headin?"

"We should really stick together. We don't know if anyone is home."

"Boy, don't be such a pussy. If dere were any bums here, we woulda seen dem by now."

"Still, we should stay close, ya know? For safety. Plus, I kind of want to see the records room, which is in one of the basements."

After a few seconds, he smirked. "Sure, bro, I get what ya mean. Tell ya what, let's go get some B-shots, and den we can go do yo nerd shit."

We laughed, and I reached out to grab the handle for the second floor, when we heard something like heavy footsteps coming from above. I shot a look at Jimmy, who was still staring at the ceiling, his camera in hand. The sound went silent just as fast as we had heard it.

"Da fuck was dat?"

"Hey man, I warned you there might be animals or people here. Maybe it was a squirrel?

"How fucking big was dat squirrel? Sounded like a damn ADHD kid running in circles up dere."

"Do you still want to head upstairs, or should we try downstairs first?"

"Naw boy, I ain't scared, let's get dis bitch on camera; shit might go viral. Plus, how many homeless peeps live in dis area? Had to have just been a bird or somethin."

While I was still trying to gather my courage, Jimmy pushed past me, grabbing the door handle and wrenching it open with a loud screech. I covered my ears with my hands, but not before we heard the footsteps running away from above us. I froze, the shadow from outside flashing in my mind. Before I could warn him, he was already through the door and halfway up the stairs.

"Jimmy! Wait!"

He ignored me. I heard the door at the top of the stairs open and close. Jimmy's steps followed the direction of those we'd heard earlier. I ran up the stairs, fear rushing through me, when I heard a muffled scream from the other side of the door. I grabbed my pocket knife and flung open the door, ready to attack whoever, or whatever, was hurting my friend. I yelled as loud as I could, bursting through the door, and saw Jimmy on the floor being licked by a dog.

"Get off me bitch! I ain't know where yo mouth been!"

I stopped, my knife raised to attack, then I burst out laughing.

"Shut up! Get this little shit off me!"

Closing my knife, I reached down and pulled the dog off of him, and it sat down, immediately wagging its tail and looking at Jimmy as he wiped the slobber off his face.

"Little shit!" Reaching down, he picked up his camera and checked it out. "This better not be fuckin broken, or else yo ass is going out da window."

The dog sat staring with its head cocked to the side, panting.

"Who are you trying to act tough with, Jim?" I said with a laugh. "You wouldn't hurt a fly. Besides, it's just a puppy."

A bit embarrassed at the comment, Jimmy shifted to look away.

"Well... Ya know what? Fuck dat dog!" he said with a dismissive wave of his hand.

"Oh, come on, it's fine."

"No, fuck you, bruh! Ya know what? Go look for yo damn filing cabinet and get da fuck out my face."

"Jeez, man, sorry."

"Just go, imma get my footage and den we gotta go, dis place sucks."

I was a little mad that he got so pissed at me over a little embarrassment, so I just threw my hands up in surrender and walked away.

"Sorry, man, I'll be downstairs when you're ready to go."

He gave me another half-assed wave. I looked around and noticed that the puppy had disappeared. *It must have wandered off*, I thought as I went back downstairs.

The door to the basement was hard to open, but eventually it gave way after I got a running start. It swung inward and created a resounding echo that bounced off the concrete walls of the dark staircase.

I rubbed my shoulder from the impact with the door and dug out my flashlight. The light seemed muted by the surfaces into a solid beam illuminating a small area in front of me. Looking out into the hall, I grabbed a piece of debris and put it in the door to keep it from closing and locking me in. Mustering up my manhood, I descended the steps carefully.

The darkness in the stairwell was unsettling. I felt cobwebs sticking to my hair and arms as I made my way down the stairs before coming to a door. Tracing the outline with the beam of my flashlight, I saw that a large bar of metal had been hastily welded into place; a handle attached to it indicated it was slid into the makeshift hasp. Not exactly a standard lock.

"Well... That doesn't seem strange at all," I said aloud, my voice echoing in the stairwell. A plaque next to the door read, "Enhanced Treatment". Pulling out the maps, I saw that my goal wasn't on the same level as the treatment rooms.

VIDEOS

I made a small mark to indicate which map was which, then I continued down the stairway. I made a mental note to bring Jimmy down here to get a few creepy shots for his vlog. That might cheer him up.

I made it to the door of basement level 2 and was shocked to see the door was already open.

"Man, I hope no one has stolen anything cool."

Checking the map again, I could see that the records room was at the end of the hall beside a room marked as "Theater."

Feeling more at ease because of the fact that the door upstairs had been almost rusted shut and it seemed clear that no one had been here for years, I stepped inside. I tried a few doors along the hall, only to find that they were all locked. The frosted glass of their windows flashed as I strafed the hall with the light. I paused the beam on the door to the records room.

The window was broken.

My hopes dipped as I approached. The broken glass was by the handle, so someone had obviously been here at some point.

Peering through the hole in the door, I could see that all the file boxes appeared to be missing. I shined the light around, and I felt a glimmer of hope when the beam reflected off of a small box.

I grabbed the handle and pushed. I felt a sharp pain hit my forehead. The door was locked, and I just slammed my head into the frame.

"Ow, goddamn it!"

Rubbing the sore spot, I reached inside and tried to turn the handle. I heard a sound from behind and spun around. Something brushed against my arm.

As I shined the light back down the hall, I swear I saw a small bipedal creature run around the corner. My body froze, knowing I wasn't alone down here, and I didn't want to shout in case it was some wild animal.

I felt something warm and wet on my hand. I played the flashlight beam over the area, and I saw a pretty large cut on my arm. It was bleeding pretty badly.

"Fuck! Well, that's not good."

Grabbing a bandanna from my backpack, I wrapped my arm. I wasn't leaving here empty-handed. As quietly as I could, I reached through the hole again and heard the satisfying click of the handle unlocking, and the door opened.

"Okay... Easy... Easy..."

Slowly I opened the door and slipped inside, closing it behind me. Letting out a sigh of relief, I slid down the door. Having a barrier between me and whatever the fuck I saw gave me reassurance that it couldn't get to me easily.

After a few seconds of collecting myself, I crawled over to the box, excitement filling my mind as I opened the cardboard flaps. The box was filled with a bunch of cameras, phones, and a few flash drives.

"This must have been some thief's storehouse for their loot."

"Find what you were looking for?"

I let out a yelp in fear and spun around to see Jimmy standing in the doorway. I had been so transfixed on my treasure I didn't even notice he had opened the door.

"Shush! I whispered."

"Huh, again with this shush shit?"

"Shush! There's something else down here."

"Dude, it's probably that stupid dog again. Come on, let's get out of here."

Standing up, I grabbed the box of goodies, and we made our way back to the exit. Reaching the ground floor, Jimmy pointed at my now blood-soaked bandage.

"Yo, you okay. bro?"

"Yeah, I'll be good, just a bad cut. Did you get your B-roll?"

"Naw, camera broke, and I got mad and threw it."

"That sucks, man. I'm sorry."

"It's fine, bro. I have another one at home. What's in the box?"

"Ironically enough, it's full of cameras," I said with a chuckle. "When I get done looking through their memory cards, I'll give ya one. It's the least I can do."

"Naw, bro. I'm good, but if there is anything awesome on them, though, let me know."

"No problem."

We made our way out of the building, and I once again felt as if I was being watched. The hairs on my arms and neck seemed to rise all at once, and I looked back over my shoulder at the building. In the dying light of the day, I thought I could see the faintest sight of that shadow from before. I stopped, and we stared at each other, and much like before, once I blinked, it was gone.

What happened in this place? I wondered.

Jimmy was a few steps ahead of me, and we walked the tracks home in silence.

Video: A walk in the woods

Opening the front door, I saw my mom in the kitchen and my stepdad still watching TV. Neither seemed to notice I had been gone all day, or that I was even home for that matter.

Well, good to see you too, guys, I'm good, by the way, just bleeding like a stuck pig, I thought as I made my way upstairs.

After plopping the old box on my bed, I went to the bathroom and untied the jerry-rigged bandage. I knew it wasn't going to be fun cleaning this gash because it was deep, but it wasn't bad enough that stitches would be needed. However, it would leave a badass scar. *Who knows, maybe it would help me with the ladies.*

I looked in the cabinet and found a bottle of rubbing alcohol with some bandages. Taking out my phone, I looked up a video on how to properly clean the now very red and hot wound.

"Shit! I hope this isn't infected. Mom will kill me, and Rob would help bury me just to get rid of me. Fuck! Okay...okay. I'll just uh...clean this out as best I can and... Umm... Hmm... In a day or two, if it gets bad, I'll just say I got jumped! No, wait, it's a small town. No way that will work. Umm, okay. I'll say on the way home, I tripped on something and got cut by some glass. Okay, that works."

Having a plan now, I grabbed the bottle, pouring the hell water over my arm. I pressed play on the video to cover the small yelp that I had to stifle. My body tensed as I screamed silently.

Jesus fucking Christ in a hooker! That hurt!

The video played, showing me how to "scrub the wound with a rough or bristled brush to help irrigate any debris or contaminants out while flushing with sterile water."

"Well shit, I need to find...uhh... There we are."

I grabbed a thin long toothbrush box, but found that it was empty. Through gritted teeth, I growled, "Okay...that's just freaking great!"

Looking down, I saw my toothbrush, and after considering the next best thing I had was toilet paper, it was pretty obvious what I needed to do.

Biting my lip, I snatched up the dirty brush and started scraping the foaming red lacerations. The pain was numbed only slightly by the adrenaline rush, but it certainly was not dulled completely. I grunted with each vigorous rub until I couldn't take it anymore. The blood, now running freely from the wound, rinsed down the drain. Grabbing a towel, I covered it and applied pressure to try and stop it from getting any worse.

"Fuck fuck fuck fuck fuck!"

Taking deep breaths, I knew I screwed up. Clutching the towel to my chest, I searched for how to close a bad cut and laughed, seeing the video of "how to use glue to seal up bad gouges."

Opening my desk drawer, I sifted through the junk until I found a small glue container. Going back to the sink, I took the bloody towel away and saw that the bleeding had finally slowed down. Pinching the cut closed, I squirted the thin liquid over the angry red line. I grunted; the pain felt like hot coals being raked over my skin. It took forever for the largest of the cuts to seal. The others weren't as bad.

Exhausted from the ordeal, I wrapped my arm and laid down on the bed next to the box. I knew there was no way to hide the injury, but even with my shitty alibi, I was pretty sure my parents wouldn't really care. I opened a bottle of ibuprofen and dry-swallowed three pills.

Closing my eyes, I felt my body relax as the pain slowly started to subside. I felt like crap, but at least it hadn't been for nothing. Looking at the box of old and new cameras, my excitement made the pain fade away even more.

Shuffling through the contents, I found a weird-looking bubble-like camera. After fiddling with it for maybe five minutes, I found the memory card and plopped it into my computer. There were a few short clips followed by one long one.

"Huh? Must not have used it too much." Clicking on the first short video, I saw that it was a video of a room. It didn't seem to have any shaking, but when I moved the cursor, the whole picture shifted, and I realized it was one of those new 360 degree cameras.

"Oh sweet, this will be cool."

Spinning the view around, an attractive woman was holding the camera while reading the instructions. In the next picture, you see her look at what I assume was the top of the camera to stop the recording.

"Cool, this must be worth some money."

The third was a video, just a quick walk-through of the girl's apartment as she was testing the audio quality. She lived in a nice place, but again it cut off after only a few minutes.

The thumbnail for the final video was of some trees. When I clicked it, the same woman was standing outside of her car; she was surrounded by a beautiful wooded area.

She said something, but the audio was muffled, and when I spun the camera, it was apparent that it was because the camera was in a protective case.

From what I could make out, it seems she was going for a nature walk to shoot a video for her parents, who couldn't physically hike anymore. The video was meant to be viewed in a virtual reality headset. Me not being a rich kid, I didn't have one, so I had to view the forest using my mouse to control the camera's orientation.

The view was beautiful. I didn't recognize the area, but wherever they were, it had amazing mountain views with fall colors adorning the trees. Her hike was spotted with parts where she would stop and take in the experience. The crunch of the leaves was like the rest of the video — muffled. A minute or two into the video, I had to mute the audio to escape the annoying sound. But the view was great.

Maybe ten minutes had passed, and I was completely engrossed in this video when it suddenly started going very fast. Thinking I'd accidentally hit the fast forward button somehow, I paused it, but when I played it again, it was still going fast. Pausing the video and spinning the camera view around, I saw that she wasn't speeding up the footage. She was running, and she was scared, given the look of terror on her face.

I searched the frozen scene but couldn't see what was chasing her. Pressing play, I watched as closely as I could. She stopped running and her head swiveled around before she bolted in a different direction. Pausing the playback again, I swung the camera to see in the direction she was facing, and I tensed, a chill running down my spine. There was a leg as if someone was hiding behind a tree, just visible for a second.

Oh shit! What am I watching? Should I be watching this? I thought about the implications of what I was seeing, but I had to know.

I hesitated briefly before pressing the button again, trying to keep an eye on whatever that figure was.

I followed the few glimpses I could catch, and the shadow of the person was huge, very clearly a man. He had to be almost seven feet tall. He moved so unbelievably fast that I could barely track him. I watched several seconds of the camera jerking in all directions until the girl looked back.

The view of the forest ended. It was replaced by gray rock speeding by. I spun the camera to see that the woman's face was contorted in a way that made my stomach churn. Then—she violently impacted the ground, her face exploding upon impact with a boulder.

Sitting in silence for a minute, I continued to watch the video. I felt my stomach lurch, and I puked into my trash can. I spun the camera away from the horrible sight of her body still twitching in its death throes.

I took a few more deep breaths after dry heaving again. Seeing that there were a few minutes left in the video, I scanned it to the end, stopping when I saw the camera move again.

Pressing play, it looked like the camera was lifted. Scanning the panorama, I stopped when the face of the large man came into view. He had some kind of mask made out of a collage of doll faces embedded directly into his skin. His eyes seemed to look over the camera before he bent down and hefted the now-dead woman's body with ease onto his shoulder. A few steps later, the video ended.

Sitting back in my chair, I felt dread, and I tried to rationalize what I had just witnessed. No way this was real. No person could move as fast as that guy had. When did he even start following her? How did the camera end up in this box?

It was some time before I could snap out of the trance-like state I found myself in, and I think the only reason I did was because I heard my mother call me down for dinner.

Having just vomited out my insides and the image of that girl's head firmly burned into my memory, I was not feeling the whole eating thing.

I shouted down that I would eat later. I knew in my current condition, they would see through whatever lie I told them. However, I felt a compulsion to re-watch the video. I wanted to see if there were any clues as to if this was just a well-done fake video, or if I had just seriously watched a woman get stalked and forced off a cliff.

Starting the video over again, it didn't take long for me to find the strange man. The woman left her car, stepping down into a ditch to make it to whatever trail she was on. Searching the area, I couldn't see much. After a minute or two passed, she made her first stop, and when I searched the background, I saw the distinct outline of the man up among the branches of a tree, pulling what looked like a body bag upward. He looked in the unaware woman's direction before hastily tying the bag in place and jumping to the ground. I was shocked that he hadn't snapped his ankles, given the height he jumped from.

Throughout the video, I watched this giant of a man move silently as he stalked this person up until she caught a glimpse of him. That's when she started running, and his unusual speed and almost acrobatic movements through the woods kept him on her tail with ease. He would be on the ground one second, then the next, he would be halfway up a tree. When the view arrived at the cliff, I turned the camera away so I didn't have to see the woman die again. The man was standing at the edge of the cliff, looking down at the camera's lens before he disappeared from the view. I reoriented the camera in the direction the man had to have come from when picking up the camera, and sure enough, I found him walking down the cliff with his face completely parallel to the ground. No wires or rope, just one slow, calm step after the other until reaching the bottom.

Stopping the video, I knew this had to have been fake. Opening up a window on my computer, I tried to narrow the search by looking for trails with mountain ranges. I spent so much time investigating that I hadn't noticed the time. The hall light flicked off, and I heard Rob and Mom go to bed.

I kept searching, and finally, I found a similar trail. It was simply called "The Point," and according to the article attached to the picture, it was a popular suicide spot. The favored methods were either hanging themselves from the tall trees or leaping to their deaths from the five-hundred-foot cliffs.

"Okay, this has to just be a school project or something. A movie made in bad taste of other people's misfortunes for shock value. Just too much unbelievable stuff. I'm just tired and need to go to bed. I'll watch the others after school tomorrow. There is just no way any of this was real."

Taking out the memory card, I put it back in the camera for safekeeping and went to bed.

Video: Watching you sleep

I tossed and turned all night, the vision of the woman's face caving in on that rock replaying in my dreams. When I opened my eyes, I could have sworn I saw the large man's masked face in my peripheral vision, only to look and it was gone. It was like that all night long.

My alarm went off, waking me to get ready for school, with all its glory until I slapped it off. Dragging myself out of bed, I went to the bathroom and checked my arm. It was incredibly bruised and puffy, but the glue seemed to hold, so after re-wrapping it, I just tried to shrug it off. Unfortunately, the soreness I felt was beyond uncomfortable. I hoped that it was just a part of the healing process.

Rifling through my clothes, I found a long sleeve shirt to cover up the bandage and made my way downstairs. Rob was sitting where my dad used to sit, eating some eggs, and mom was making some more for me.

I was still kind of delirious from the lack of sleep as I sat at the table, my brain not processing that I was awake. I accidentally spilled one of their drinks when I reached for the salt. Rob stood up abruptly, yelling and causing my mom to flinch. It was like he was just waiting for me to screw up, shouting , "You are such a waste of time" and to just "Go upstairs until the school bus shows up." Not wanting to argue, I just grabbed some dry toast and went upstairs again.

Lightly slamming my door shut, I still had time to grab another memory card from the box and have a look.

Sifting through its contents, I found an almost-new phone with a cracked screen.

Oh nice, I can use this.

Pressing the power button, I was surprised to see the screen light up. The indicator showed that quite a bit of battery was left. I slid the screen to open the phone, expecting some sort of lock screen, but it opened to the main screen. I punched the icon for messages and looked at the most recent texts. Apparently, this person had recently lost this phone, maybe a few months ago. Going off the way the conversations were worded, I guessed that it was some guy's phone, and the subsequent selfies seemed to back up that assumption.

"Get your ass down here. You're gonna be late to school."

"Screw you," I mumbled under my breath.

Shoving the phone in my pocket, I ran downstairs and out to the bus. I spent the whole trip swiping through some of the photos. This guy seemed to really like Halloween decorations. I was about to reset the phone when I saw a security app notification.

Tapping the app took me to a screen with a very long list of "movement alert notifications." They were all over the course of a few days, all with video or pictures attached to them.

"Hey!"

My attention was pulled away from the phone to see Jimmy walking up the bus aisle, tossing his backpack into the seat in front of me. He sat so that he could see me, and he seemed kind of worried about something.

"Yo, how's your arm?"

As distracted as I had been by the phone's contents, I hadn't been paying attention to it. I felt it, and thought that it felt kind of warm.

"It was rough cleaning it, but it should be fine." *I hope...*

"Good, good, yo, so I was wondering if you got a visit from our buddy last night?"

"Buddy?"

"Yeah, that stupid dog followed me home last night and was chillin outside my window just staring at me the whole time."

"Okay? So the dog followed your smell, not like you're hard to track from that."

"I don't know, bro. Something seemed off, though. I tried shouting at it to screw off and even threw a ball. And nothing. The dog just sat there. There was just something unsettling with its eyes. It looked like it was studying me. It was fucking weird. It must have lost interest, though, because I fell asleep, and when I woke up, it was gone."

It took me a second, but then it dawned on me: I could understand everything Jimmy had just said. I wondered if he was okay, or maybe if this whole dog thing scared him for real.

Or it could be that my arm was making me delirious, and broken internet language now automatically translated for me. I said, "Maybe you scared it off."

"Dat's the otha weird part. It didn't even flinch. Even when I threw da ball, it was like a statue when it bounced right next to it."

Oh, there it was. He must have just had a moment of clarity.

"I had a weird night myself, but no dog involved."

"What happened to you?"

"Well, after taking care of my arm, I went through that box, and it turns out, all the stuff in there is like cameras and phones and shit."

Taking out the phone, I explained to Jimmy what I saw on the memory card last night. I started to tell him that I found another odd series of alerts on this phone, but the bus stopped to let us off. We decided to meet up at lunch and study hall to watch the notifications and maybe see if there was a home invasion or something.

Sitting through my classes, it just felt like time was slowing down with random speed-ups. One minute it was like the big hand had something holding it down, but when I looked away and back again, it was as if a spring was set to go off, shooting it forward by a half hour.

I sat in my chair, every so often checking to make sure the phone was still in my pocket. On a few occasions, the teacher almost caught me, but she didn't seem very interested. She would just roll her eyes and continue with the lesson.

When the bell rang for lunch, I must have been almost running to get to the cafeteria because I was one of the first people there. I found the table I usually sat at with Jimmy and started going through the still-shot photos.

The first few pictures were of a living room and a bedroom, with a short man just standing in the rooms. His face was obscured by the shadows, but I assumed that it must be the owner. The last few images for that night just showed the guy walking through the house and standing in each room for up to an hour or more before disappearing back into someplace in the living room, according to the timestamps.

Looking up, I saw Jimmy in line. I continued flipping through the man's pictures . There appeared to be another guy returning to the apartment, and the thought occurred to me. This guy has a full head of hair. Switching to the security pictures again, the short man in them was bald.

"What the fu...?"

"Hey, Squeaks! Hope you didn't start without me?"

A little confused, I looked up at Jimmy as he sat down and scootched up next to me, the faint smell of corn chips wafting from him.

"What? No, I was just looking through the pictures, but check this out." Then I added, "Don't call me 'Squeaks.'"

Clicking through, I showed Jimmy the owner and then the few pictures I found of the strange bald man.

"Must be a robber," Jimmy said.

"Maybe, but where's the owner, and where did this guy go?"

"How da hell should I know?" he said with a laugh. "Maybe he just wasn't home, and this creeper was waiting up for him."

"Well, there are three videos on the list. Maybe they'll answer the questions."

"Well, don't keep me in suspense bitch, hit dem buttons."

I was a little put off by Jimmy's excitement, but I found the first video and tapped play.

The video was mute. It showed the owner of the phone doing his nightly routine, I'm guessing. Walking through the house. The feed followed him to his kitchen where he grabbed a beer before continuing on. The footage switched from room to room following his movements. The house appeared set up for Halloween, and he seemed to stop in his living room and randomly slapped something off-camera, laughing a bit as he did so. It wasn't too unnerving; however, after the hit, he turned around, flipped off the lights, and went to bed.

Not too long after, the camera turned on in the living room, as a box holding something fell over from that same area the owner had slapped. The timestamp showed an hour had passed since then, and nothing seemed to run on camera to explain why the box fell.

The view switched to the bedroom, where the owner's phone glowed at its resting spot on the nightstand. It must have triggered the camera in the bedroom to start recording. We watched as the phone went dark in the video, and not long after, the camera switched back to the living room. But now a hand was visible in the corner of the screen. Then, back to the bedroom as the phone's lit screen was again clearly visible. This back-and-forth continued over the course of several hours, though nothing seemed to have moved in the living room.

When the guy woke up in the morning, he seemed annoyed when he saw how many notifications he'd received. He went to the living room, looked about, then moved to the edge of the viewing field. He stood up whatever had fallen during the night, waving a hand in its direction as if dismissing the object of his attention as he walked away.

He must have switched the video to a still camera or something because the only options for the next day were the pictures I had already looked at.

The next series of pictures were very similar to the last. However, Jimmy and I stopped on the first bedroom picture where the bald man could be seen standing in the doorway while the owner was fast asleep in bed. His phone lit up with the notifications.

"Yo dude... dis is getting creepy. I don't know if I want to see the next few pictures."

I slid to the next few pictures, and this unknown man was now stepping into the room and eventually standing over the owner. The next picture in the notifications was three hours later, and the pictures following showed the bald guy going back to the blind spot, and finally of the owner waking up.

There were only two videos left, but before we could start watching, the bell rang for our next class. It was the longest hour of my life as I sat there in anticipation, just wanting to know what else was caught on video. My curiosity finally got to be too much, so I raised my hand to use the bathroom. I found an empty stall, locked the door, and clicked the next video.

It started like the last one with the guy going through his nightly routine, but in this video, the living room contained a box with what looked like a body hanging out of it.

I paused the video. It looked like the box was labeled as a full-sized person decoration. It was oddly crammed into the box, but nothing seemed to be off other than the familiar bald head.

"No... No way."

The video played out, and the whole time, I kept telling myself, "Don't let that thing move" on a loop in my head.

After the owner fell asleep, the camera switched its view, and stayed in the living room. I watched closely, focused on the mannequin, until my heart jumped. Its hand began to move on its own. It was slow and methodical, but it was moving. Just like before, the camera started to switch between the bedroom and the living room, and each time it switched, there was something different. The body was now tipped over and was working itself out of the box. Its boneless body twisted and contorted to better slide out of its confinement.

The view flipped to the owner in the bedroom again, then quickly back to the now-standing figure. The body seemed to move before its head and arms, which seemed to glide behind it as it slowly made its way through the house. Each labored step was followed by the creepy swaying head and arms. It took almost forty-five minutes, but finally the doll-like silhouette stood motionless in the doorway again, with the owner still fast asleep and completely unaware of the situation.

All this time, I could see the man's phone flashing alerts until the man woke up and shut it off. This deranged-looking prop was now standing only a few feet behind him.

He laid back down and appeared to fall asleep again, and now the figure moved closer, again leaning over the poor man. For an anxiety-ridden hour of video, it just stood there watching him sleep.

Suddenly, it snapped forward, grabbed the man's neck, and began choking and hitting the horrified man. Seconds passed like minutes before the doll started tearing chunks out of his struggling victim, its emotionless face and head just waving in all directions. It was only a matter of minutes before this assault was over.

Tearing my eyes away, I was glad I was in the bathroom because I felt myself about to shit at the video.

Looking back, the horrific scene was still displayed, and the doll was now pulling the man's face off, wrapping it around its own head as a crude fleshy mask, before calmly hobbling over to the nightstand and grabbing the phone. Minutes later, it walked back into the living room as if nothing had happened. It squeezed itself back into the box. The room brightened as the sun came up and shone through the windows. The rest of the video switched to the view of the bedroom as the man's body occasionally twitched with death rattles before finally ending.

I walked to my study hall in silence, not realizing the phone was still gripped tightly in my hand. Jimmy ran up to me, and his voice was a muffled mess. He seemed overly excited to see the video. I told him it wouldn't be smart for him to see it and just sat there, zoned out, the rest of the day. By the time I zoned back in, I was home and had several missed texts from Jimmy wanting to know what happened to me and why I left school early.

I didn't know how to respond, but I understood that what I was in possession of was clear evidence of some sort of paranormal murders. It took a few minutes to work myself out of the fog that was my mind, and I realized I was still holding the phone, and there was a recent notification from that day. It was a video that had been activated while I was in class, but since the phone was on silent, I hadn't noticed it was new.

Clicking the video, it showed the doll again, its new face now rotted and falling apart, maggots crawling all over it. Seconds later, what I assumed to be the owner's front door exploded inward, and two very surprised police officers entered the room and instantly covered their mouths. They fought through their revulsion and went back into clearing mode. Guns drawn, they made their way to the bedroom, discovering the gory scene. When they left the bedroom after radioing it in, the camera followed them from room to room.

When they walked past the doll, its head turned to follow them out the door before the video stopped again.

Placing the phone on my nightstand, I laid down and went through my options. On one hand, I had videos showing and proving people were killed by mysterious monsters. On the other hand, I was in possession of proof of creepy monsters killing people, and there is no way in hell any sane police officer would ever believe me — even with the videos — that they were real.

VIDEOS

The thought of what my few options were kept me awake, but I eventually made my choice.

I thought about it. I thought long and hard, but in the end, I made the only sensible and logical choice that kept me out of the loony bin.

Video: Crawlspace

The only option I had was to keep these videos as evidence. Still, I couldn't go to the police because I would be arrested for theft and trespassing as well as trying to submit a fake report, if they didn't just assume I was crazy. I also didn't want to go back to that asylum any time soon to put these back where I'd found them.

So I now faced an even weirder question... Should I finish watching the rest of these? Again, it was possible that these videos were just some film school kids' projects; with the editing software available, some of these could have been done in a week or two.

I had been sitting there for quite a while that morning, trying to best logic out whether I should keep the videos and watch them. I managed to convince myself that once I watched all of them, I should just drop the box off with a note at the police station.

"Yeah... Yeah, that's the plan then."

I shot a text off to Jimmy explaining that the reason I left school was because I wasn't feeling well. He sent a "sigh" response and wanted to know if he could come over and watch the rest of the video.

Freezing at the thought that he might take it and run, I told him I'd give him the phone, but I would need it back when I turned the box in to the police. He gave me an exaggerated "fine" and said he would be over later to pick it up. I wasn't too sure about whether or not I should let him see it, but decided that maybe it was for the best, if for no other reason than so someone else can see and I was able to verify I was not crazy.

Looking at the time, I went back to the box and found an action camera covered in mud. Its protective case was also in the box but seemed to have been crushed. It was weird since that type of case was meant to be damn near unbreakable, but here it was, splintered apart like someone smashed it with a sledgehammer. The camera itself was fine, albeit pretty dirty.

Checking the camera out, I found the USB charge port and decided, against my better judgment, to plug it into my computer. After the software finished uploading, a screen popped up. The screen showed a long list of pictures from a confined area. Someone in a muddy yellow hazmat suit and a mask was wedged into this area. The last of the pictures was a video. Double-clicking it, I instantly paused it, because this video, unlike the others, had clear audio.

Plugging in my headphones, not knowing what to expect and not wanting my parents to hear, I pressed play again and just listened and watched.

"HELLO, HELLO, THIS thing on?" the man said, tapping the camera. He seemed to be an older guy, maybe mid-to-late-thirties. He began putting on the banana-yellow protective suit over his uniform, then he fit a respirator over his face. A younger-looking guy with a less-than-enthused look on his face stood next to him.

"Okay, kid, ready for your first crawlspace?"

The younger guy didn't look very comfortable. He just said, "Oh yeah. Overjoyed," in the driest sarcastic tone I had ever heard. It made me laugh a little.

The camera shifted, as the older guy placed it onto a harness affixed to his suit. Sweat dripped down the younger man's face as they trudged toward a small house on a beach. The video feed from the chest-mounted camera showed sand surrounding this cute little house, with some sparse grass growing where it could.

A rough sketch of a rectangle on a blue folder popped into the camera's view when the man stopped walking.

"Are you fucking kidding me?" he said in a very annoyed tone. "This fucking guy is useless."

"What's up?" the younger man said, confused.

"Well, look at the house." The older man gestured toward the structure. The younger man's eyes followed his hand. "Now look at the moisture map. The shit isn't a rectangle now, is it?"

Realizing their predicament, the younger man dropped his shoulders and looked up to the sky, mimicking the elder's mood.

"Listen, we don't know what it looks like down there. I'm gonna need you to stay by the entry, and I'll explore in there to find out what the real situation is. If I need help, I'll shout out to you what I'll need. Okay?"

Both men stared at the entrance to the crawlspace. The younger guy nodded in agreement, then he quickly removed the top portion of his suit, stating, "It's too damn hot to be wearing this shit!"

"Fair enough. Let's get this started, shall we?" the older man said before approaching the small trap door set in the floor of a closet.

The older man opened the door and entered the dark hole. After only a few steps, the camera was below the floor and showed the dirt- and sand-floored crawlspace. The cinder block-enclosed room was rectangular; however, just to the right of the entry, another hole was visible in the camera's dimly-lit view. Some sort of trench drained a black tar-like substance into a sub-pump.

"This room's dry," he called. With an audible sigh, the man began crawling through the hole into another space, which appeared to be a side portion under the house. The three-foot-tall height to the ceiling in the first space seemed to be cut in half in this new room. His grunts were accompanied by the slight sloshing sound of whatever was in the trench.

Suddenly he stopped and tried to point the camera at something. The camera was angled down, and was now trapped between the muddy floor and the suit. The light fluttered around the space, illuminating the area in several places.

The older man said, "Well, shit..." Then, louder, "Okay. Hey kid! Grab me the hose and get the truck started. I gotta tuck in here and get to the back section."

The video was quiet other than the sound of the man's breathing. Another sound became apparent – the faint sound of a baby crying. The man didn't seem to notice the cry before the sound of a loud engine roared to life, snuffing it out to the point of being inaudible. A big vacuum hose appeared from behind the man, and then the camera began moving again with the now-steady sound of the strong suction.

The area seemed to become more and more cramped as the man crawled further, periodically stopping to suck up chunky sewage from the deeper portions of the trench. The hose extended in front of him, ensuring that the path was clear as he moved forward; its suction removing foul debris amid gulps of air and water. The consistent slurping noises were punctuated by thumps as chunks of solid waste were vacuumed through the tube and back to the tank. The man paused whenever he hit an area of water, waiting for the tube to do its job.

Finally, he came to a space which was essentially a room measuring around a hundred square feet. The space was less claustrophobic-appearing, with a floor-to-ceiling height of maybe two to three feet. "Oh well...that's just a bunch of sexy right there now, isn't it?" the man said, looking at this large kiddie pool-sized area filled with someone else's shit.

After plunging the end of the hose into the pool, he just seemed to lay still. But as he rested, the distinctive sound of a crying child could be heard in the background. As he recorded his audio notes on the five separate subsections of the crawlspace, he added "Now, if someone could just shut this freaking kid up, this might be an easier job."

The video was pretty uneventful except for the constant crying, which only seemed to grow louder and louder, almost as if it was in competition with the vacuum's engine. The older man just kept on talking as the hose did its dirty job, muttering every few minutes that "This kid needs to shut the fuck up." Eventually, he managed to suck up almost all of the chunky soupy mess in the area. That was when he discovered a thick membrane under all the nastiness.

"Huh, that's an odd plastic," he said. He pulled it up and the camera showed that it covered several very round objects which might have been stones.

Looking around, he must have seen another puddle of sewage, because he looked down again, seemingly searching for another way around that did not involve crawling over the rocks. Apparently, given the look of defeat in his eyes, he wasn't successful.

He began to move again. He groaned as he painfully crawled across the uncomfortable surface. At least the sudden increase in height in the short space allowed him to squat instead of crawling through the nasty substance on his belly. The whole time he was crossing the stones, the crying was very loud and insistent. It sounded as if it was coming from within the room he was in.

Finally, he managed to make it to the other end of the space. However, as soon as he plunged the head of the vacuum hose into the thick liquid, the sounds of the engine and the crying went silent.

"That crying must have been the truck," he said to himself, his mask now slightly fogged by the humidity.

The voice of the younger guy could be heard as he hollered down the hatch about the machine shutting down. "Drain the tank!" he shouted back. Several minutes of silence passed as he waited, and then his flashlight started to flicker. "God damn it! Why do they always buy us the cheapest shit to use?" Flicking it off to save power, he waited for the kid to return to the hole to get a new light source.

Not too long after the light went out, the sound of the truck leaving was only made worse by the small slivers of light making it to the back corners where the older man sat, annoyed. Suddenly, the muffled sound of the crying returned.

"That's just freaking wonderful," he said, kicking one of the larger round rocks. The sound became clearer for a split second. "What the hell?"

He turned his flashlight back on, lifted his leg, and kicked the small boulder. Then he grabbed it with both hands and began to raise it up. The camera only caught a glimpse before falling to the ground again, and the man, suddenly screaming expletives while crawling backward, his light still trained on the partially flipped rock.

SQUINTING TO GET A better look, I leaned into the screen and tried to see what was so scary, but all I could make out were what looked like *worms* attached to the bottom of the stone, that was until it started rising out of the ground. A segmented body wriggled up violently from the mud. I heard the man's scream on the playback as he began to move, but the cries were drowning out whatever he was saying. This unknown creature slapped down, splashing the gross liquid across the lens of the camera repeatedly as more of it worked itself free.

It was joined by countless others tearing through that weird membrane from below.

I tried to see more details, but the man started scrambling and the video became jerky and blurred. When it stabilized momentarily, I could see that one of the nightmare-fueled monsters had latched onto his shoulder. I saw it rear back, opening its underside revealing thousands of worm-like legs, each tipped with spine-like grippers. Its whole body cavity opened up like a Venus Fly Trap, and it slammed down onto whatever part of his uniform that the camera was attached to, blacking out the video. Thrashing sounds mixed with the man's terrified pleas for help were audible as the camera flew across the screen, landing near the small opening he would have to crawl to in order to survive. It faced into the room, so I could see all of the grizzly details of what happened next.

There were so many of them, all different sizes but all the same color and shape. They ganged up on him as he grabbed blindly for anything to pull himself free. His suit was torn and bloody from the few that latched on before he could rip them away.

From the right of the camera's lens, a much larger creature slid out from behind another hole in a wall. Its body was being pushed along by what looked like a baby's legs. Black slime oozed from its body as it went. The man, now on his butt and facing the smaller monsters, was unknowingly moving towards the bigger one as he tried to get away completely unaware of the danger. Mentally, I was screaming for the poor man to just turn around and see what was coming.

Kicking off the last small one, he whipped around, crawling with all his strength only to stop and look up slowly as the large creature blocked the already- obscured view. The man's screams became muffled, then his voice was silenced.

Silence, except for the wails of the screaming babies.

The segmented body of the larger creature undulated away as several of the smaller monstrosities dragged the man's body back into the strange pit. A few minutes passed as the pit started to fill back up again with that strange black substance.

Even though the whole situation was disturbing, once the pool filled again, all the creatures were gone, and it looked as if nothing had ever happened. Even the screaming babies were now silent.

Like the other videos, the video continued to record. I sat listening for anything that could show this was fake, but at this point, I was beginning to think these weren't fake anymore.

Eventually, I heard the dull hum of the truck returning from dumping the waste. My heart raced, knowing what had just happened.

"Yo, you okay down there, old man?" the younger guy shouted.

"Please don't go down there. Please just turn around and walk away." I knew it was pointless, but I still mumbled it to myself for a sense of security.

"What the fuck?" The camera lifted, and I could see the young man's face and the look of confusion written all over his face. After looking around and shouting out his co-worker's name a few times, he began crawling his way out.

After crawling back into the dry area, the sound of the muffled cry started again. The last part of the video was the young man lifting the camera and from the other side of the room behind him was one of those creatures crawling out from the trench. His last words on the recording were, "There's the off button." After that, the screen went black.

I sat there re-watching the video, looking for anything that might indicate CGI was used, or an indication of strings or puppetry being employed, but I couldn't find anything.

My phone started to vibrate, and it was Jimmy letting me know he was here. I grabbed the phone and went down to meet him.

He was still very excited to see the videos, but I warned him that I didn't think these were fake.

"Yo, man. Don't worry. I got this." That was all he said before hopping on his bike and racing off.

I started to feel a bit woozy and laid down. I knew I would pass out, and I hoped that the things I'd seen wouldn't work their way into my sleep.

Within a few minutes, I was gone and into my dream world.

Video: Shadows

I woke up to the sound of my phone exploding with texts. Rubbing the tired eye snot from my eyes, I looked out the window and saw that it was still dark. Snatching up my phone, I saw that it was 3 am, and the number of missed messages was astounding. I didn't recall ever having had this many messages in years. Some were from people I hadn't spoken to in months.

But most were from Jimmy.

Reading through, it seemed like he was way more entertained by the video than I thought he would be. He went on and on about how real it looked, and then I saw what I was hoping I wouldn't see. "It was so cool. I posted it to my channel, and da shit went viral."

Bolting awake, I went straight to his channel, and the views were nearing a hundred thousand.

"Oh my god, that stupid fuck!"

I texted him back: , "What the fuck were you thinking?"

His response was just as simple as I thought it would be. "For da money, bro, that one video just made us at least five-hundred dollars, and I plan on sharing that shit with you too."

"We don't even know if it's real or fake! If that's real, you just posted a murder online. Not cool at all!" I typed as fast I could, begging him to take it down.

"Bro, it can't be real. Dolls don't just come to life and kill people. Plus, clearly, these are fake, just really good effects. Dude, trust me, dese could be our money ticket."

I put my phone down, and it did start to make a little sense. I couldn't shake the feeling that these were all fake. *If what I just watched was true, then we would have seen these things all over the place, right?*

VIDEOS

Standing up, I went to the window and stared out in contemplation. *What's the harm? I mean, if they are fake, then the original creators would come forward to take credit, right? And if they are real, someone is bound to step forward to identify the victims. It's kind of a self-fixing issue at that point, right? Then if the police ask, we can just say we found them; we found them and thought they were fake, and now we have plausible deniability.*

Thinking it through, I sent a message to Jimmy. "If we post these videos, I'm going to watch them first just to be on the safe side, but if anyone comes forward as the victim's families or the creators, we have to do the right thing and take the videos down."

It only took a few seconds before I got his response, "Fo sho, dude, but in the meantime, let's just enjoy a little extra coin in our pockets."

Reluctantly, I had to agree with him. Plus, with the school year coming to an end, I could use that money to get the hell out of this house.

Going back to the window, I was about to close the blinds when I noticed a weird figure standing outside. I squinted to try and see it better. It looked like a small person standing just out of the light of the street lamp. Its shadow was thin and sickly, but whatever it was, it didn't look human to me. When it finally started taking shape, it leaned forward into the light, went down onto all fours, and ran into the illuminated area. Now, I could see it was the dog from the asylum. The little dog took one look up at me standing in the window and ran off into the night.

Guess it was just the dog standing on its hind legs, I thought. As odd as that thought was, given the events of the last few days, it didn't seem too out of the ordinary to me. I checked the clock in my room and noticed that it was almost 4 am. I still had school in the morning.

THE DAY STARTED THE same as always. Rob had his nose in the paper, and Mom was doing whatever she was doing. I wasn't sure what I expected, but obviously, they wouldn't even notice if I did become famous for anything.

Grabbing my computer, I said "Fuck it," and reached into the box again, this time finding a flash drive. It seemed like a good day to skip school. I figured everyone would be talking about the video anyways, and I didn't need the replays being shown all day to me. Seeing it once was enough.

I snuck away after walking out the door, and the bus just continued past the house as if I were sick. *Even the school doesn't care if I'm there or not,* I thought to myself. I wasn't going to school, but I knew where I *was* going: the train station.

Walking through the tall grass, the feeling of being watched washed over me. *It must be my imagination,* I thought, but I still felt the unease as if I was being followed. The odd quiet sound of distant bugs traveled through the clearing, only to become virtually silent around me. With each step, the circle of silence moved with me like a looming cloud before a rainstorm. Every step I took felt as if it had a small, light echo. The sound of my feet hitting the ground seemed off, almost like the steps were out of sequence.

"It's all in your head. Just relax. No one's following you." Even my voice sounded weird to my ears.

Closing my eyes, I took a breath, and as the air left my chest, I heard a twig snap. My eyes shot open and I ran as fast as I could.

Branches and weeds slapped my face and tore at my clothes until I ran chest-first into the ledge of the old terminal. I felt all the life in me burst out with a sudden sharp exhale.

I lay on the ground gasping for breath when I heard footsteps behind me. I scrambled to face my attacker, holding my computer like a nerdy club.

The bushes rattled as whatever it was charged out. It was a blur of brown and tan. I fell on my back, landing hard on the old rail, and screamed for help, but my calls were cut short by a fury of wet licks to my face.

It was that fucking dog. "Get off of me! Fuck off, ya little shit!" It took a few seconds, but I was able to finally push it off.

"Go sit over there!" I shouted as I wiped the slobber off my face.

I looked back at the dog after brushing myself off. Its head was cocked to the side as if it didn't understand why I was wiping off its kisses.

"Stupid dog, scaring me and shit! No wonder you were abandoned." Stepping up onto the platform, I pulled out the flash drive and angrily shoved it into the port on the computer.

Looking down at the puppy's eyes, I was still annoyed, but its fuzzy face and stupid tongue hanging out made it very hard to be mad at it. "You better hope you didn't break my damn computer, or else I'm taking you to the nice Chinese restaurant up the road. They'll make Pai-kin Puppy out of you."

Standing up, I collected myself with the stupid look on the dog's face following my every move. "You want something?"

Again, it just sat there panting in response, tail wagging away. "Whatever!"

A series of pictures of shadows without people to cast them loaded up. The last thumbnail was for a video d that appeared to be of a news anchor from a different country sitting at the desk. Chinese or Japanese lettering filled the screen behind her. It was labeled "Unaired Footage."

"Well... Here we go."

I clicked it and the video instantly started. At first, it showed very old black and white footage. There was no audio, but then the label "Taken at Detonation Site" scrolled across the top. A second text bar appeared, stating "TOP SECRET Hiroshima/Nagasaki."

"This one must be from World War 2," I said, looking towards the dog. It responded with a slight sigh, and laid down.

A few turns of the camera revealed several destroyed buildings, either collapsed or blown to pieces. There were shadows projected against them, and the ground was spattered with random ones. At one point, I swear I even saw one of the shadows move.

The video jumped to a different area, and it showed a few people running from something, only to be stopped randomly and then dragged against the ground to the walls where they were carried up as high as they could go. Then they were dropped from that height. This happened several times in some cases until the person was dead.

"What the hell is this now?" Looking at the video length, it was only a few minutes long, but I had to know what had just killed those people.

The video jumped again. This time, it showed a very bright white room with several humanoid-looking shapes against the wall, moving exceptionally fast. *Wait...No... Not against it, they were the wall! Were those the shadows from the street?*

Another jump showed the shadows attacking a group of guards, pulling them to the ground and literally tearing them apart. It was as if it was some sick feeding-frenzy. Wherever blood or body parts hit the ground, a shadow would slither over to it and dissolve whatever it could into its dark mass.

The camera jerked and was pulled several feet before it was dragged up a wall. A few seconds passed, and the camera fell to the ground with the lens now facing up towards the ceiling. A spray of black liquid coated the ceiling. In an instant, several of the shadows converged on the black splatter, making it disappear as if it had never been there.

"What the fuck?" I was awestruck and started wondering how such creatures could exist. Were they the souls of the victims after the bombs dropped? Or something else?

The clip abruptly switched to a Japanese newscaster. It appeared to be a more modern recording. I couldn't understand a word of what she was saying, so I took out my phone and used a pocket translator app to get the gist of her words.

I ran the video back and held up my phone to input the audio into the app. It read out, "The video you just watched was recovered from a time capsule that was unearthed this year. We have other clips from the other cameras that appeared to have been buried as if to hide them. We here at the network have sent them for authentication and have discovered they are all real. Viewer discretion is advised; the videos contain graphic content."

The video shifted a bit, and another clip began to play. A group of men armed with floodlights ran into a dark building and began saturating the rooms with light so bright it almost seemed to fry the lens of the camera.

The walls were black, and moving shadows were visible in the video, running in all directions. The old black and white footage shifted again, and the video jumped to a man holding a long staff, which had some strange-looking electronics attached haphazardly along the shaft. The camera panned to the right and a small cell lit up except for a small area of the room about the size of a floor tile.

The man entered the room and flipped a switch on the staff. The end began to glow.A dark filter was placed over the lens of the camera. As the brightness became stronger, the wielder flipped down what looked like an old-fashioned welder's hood, and jammed the staff into the darkened spot.

The bright white end then clasped shut around something in the room, and a struggle ensued until another man came from behind the camera to help the first guy.

Between the two of them, they managed to pull the shadowy demon from the room into the light. As it was forced from the corner, the darkness drained as more was pulled free. I watched its body disintegrate as it was exposed to the brightness. Soon, another man armed with another light staff grabbed another limb of the creature, and all three at once yanked and pulled the creature away from the wall, its body instantly thrashed until finally dissipating. The three men cheered and congratulated each other.

The next clip showed a large building that looked like a power plant. A man was taking a camera crew in to show what was going on. The first few minutes showed nothing out of the ordinary, until they exited an elevator.

VIDEOS

Before the doors opened, the lead man handed everyone a welding hood, and another dark lens was placed over the lens of the camera.

The doors opened to another brightly lit hallway. Doors lining each side, and a man in a full radiation suit stood guard next to a large red button. I couldn't read the sign, but according to the translator, it was along the lines of "Press in case of escape, Cover eyes!"

Stopping at a doorway, the cameraman looked inside to see the room was dark – the blackest black I had ever witnessed. A door behind the guard opened and another similarly dressed man pushed a cart laden with rods of some sort into the hall.

The man proceeded to stop at each door, opened a small hole, and fed the rods into the dark rooms. Occasionally hitting red buttons on the side of the doorways before moving on.

When the cart made it to the film crew, they documented the man placing the rod into the hole and watched as shadowed hands grabbed hold, making it seem to be floating in the air. Some unintelligible words were spoken, and the cart man hit the red button along the door. The room flooded with light for a few seconds before resuming its darkened state. When the camera refocused, the rod lifted to the ceiling and then evaporated into the wall.

"Are those fuel rods? Are they using these things as some sort of radioactive disposal thing?" I questioned, not expecting an answer.

The video then cut back to the anchor, who now looked very frightened. A red splatter was behind where her co-anchor had been sitting. She was breathing heavily as a gunshot was heard, and the camera slumped down, pointing at an angle to the floor.

A pair of non-descript legs walked into view, and a large box was wheeled by the frame.

I could hear the woman begging for her life before another gunshot silenced her. A few seconds passed, then a heavy lock could be heard being released as a bright glow lit up the floor. An audible "clink" could be heard, and a man's voice said, "feeding time" before the video cut to black.

I sat back after the video ended and just took in the insanity. Was that what I saw in the asylum? "That was intense. I wonder if that's going on here in our power plants."

Taking out my phone, I texted Jimmy to come meet me after school; I had another video for him.

I looked around but saw that the dog was gone now. Maybe it went to roll around in a dead animal or something. I just knew, though, that I had to go before it came back. I didn't want it following me home.

Video: Daddy issues

The walk from the old terminal was seriously unnerving now that apparently I had to watch my own shadow. The thought of being torn apart and pulled into some strange dimension to be devoured by it was one that I never foresaw having, but here we are.

I headed to the school after texting Jimmy. He said he wanted to get the next video up as soon as possible. According to him, "dem shit's been more viral than a ghetto hoe at da club."

With a heavy sigh and already regretting my choice to share the videos, I plodded on. I was hoping he didn't get too pushy; I've seen how he gets when he gets some success.

I waited for him near the cafeteria, and surprisingly, he wasn't late.

"Yo dude, you got the shit?" Jimmy walked over, swaggering more with each step as he got closer. It sounded more like we were doing a drug deal than swapping videos. The look on his face was pure happiness.

"Yes, Jimmy, I have the video. It's a good one too, definitely some paranormal stuff in this one. When can I expect my cut?"

His stance changed to what I knew he called 'business casual.' Basically, he stood there,hand still in pants pockets, leaning back like some drug dealer. His smile was still as shit-eating as ever. "Oh, don't worry about dat, bro. I got you covered."

"You better," I said. :These videos are getting more and more twisted, and I don't have many left."

He lowered his shoulders a bit, and his stance relaxed. "Trust me, bro, with dese bennies coming in from dees vids, we be good for a while."

Looking him up and down, I had a feeling something was up, but I had other shit to deal with. "Okay, dude, just catch up with me when the money comes in, alright?"

"No prob, bro. Just hit me up wit dat next vid, and we be good." With that, he threw up his hands, "Deuces!" And went back inside.

"Deuces?" What the hell? I hadn't heard that in, like, ever, from him. *Guess he's trying to "bring it back."* Whatever. It wasn't the time for that.

I still had some time, though. *Maybe I can get another video in. Rob is probably at work, and Mom is probably passed out in a wine coma, so if I'm gonna get another video, I'll have to swing by there.*

The uneventful walk home was quicker than expected, and I was happy to see that Rob's car wasn't in the driveway. Sneaking around to the windows, I saw that Mom had passed out for her afternoon "nap" with her favorite adult juice box lying next to her.

"What a winner," I mumbled. Sneaking around back, I went inside and headed up to my room. The box was still there, but something was off. There were only three cameras left. "Where the fuck did they all go?" Looking around the room, I couldn't find any trace of the missing cameras. I felt a breeze, and I looked towards the window. A dirty hand-print and a paw print were on the sill and floor.

"Are you kidding me? Some asshole robbed me!" Looking around, I realized that nothing was missing other than the files and the camcorders.

"Why the hell... JIMMY!" That piece of shit! Grabbing my phone, I furiously started texting him.

"WHY THE FUCK DID YOU STEAL THOSE VIDEOS!"

His return text was almost immediate. "Boy, you actin cray-cray? I've been at school all day squeaky, the fuck you on about?"

"Someone broke into my room and stole the videos!"

"Shit, boy. What da fuck we gonna do now?"

I didn't know what to say. The only thing I could think to do was maybe go back to the asylum and hope for the best. But in the meantime, I had to give him something.

"Tell ya what, I still have three of these things left. I'll watch the next one, and tomorrow, I'll head over to the asylum. There has to still be something there to get some content."

A few minutes passed as I waited for him to respond. Walking over to the window, I started to close it when I looked down to see that dog sitting in the middle of the road again. It was looking up at me, and I was entranced by its eyes. Slowly I reached up and locked the window. The click of the latch gave me some comfort.

I continued to watch as the dog stood up and began walking towards the front door. Its eyes and head never broke its gaze into my eyes. Even as it was right under me, I still felt it staring.

I gotta get out of here, I thought, grabbed the box, and headed to the staircase.

When I got to the top of the stairs, I looked down and saw that the front door was open.

"What the...? How did it open the door?" Sneaking down the steps, I kept my eyes peeled, and I froze when I saw the dog sitting in the living room staring at my mother. It hadn't seen me yet, so I just had to make it to the door. Then I could call animal control or whoever to help my mom.

I stood there waiting, but it just sat there like a statue. Almost as if it was *taxidermied*, it was so still. I took a few more tentative steps when I felt and heard the step creak under my weight.

Instantly the dog's eye shifted and it was now staring at me, though its face still looked at my mother. I was terrified; the way it was looking at me was so unnatural. Its mouth opened, and its tongue stretched down and out of its mouth. Slowly it leaned towards the sleeping woman. The whole time, its eye tracked me as it leaned in and started to lick her face.

I was terrified and made a choice to run for it. *I'll call for help or get a cop or someone. I am not fucking with that weird-ass dog.* Running to the doorway, I grabbed the handle, slamming the door behind me. I heard my mother scream, and I took off running, box in hand.

When I felt I was far enough, I grabbed my phone just as it vibrated with a message. "Sounds like a plan, my dude. Maybe I'll join ya."

Leaning up against a house, I felt like I was hidden, so I called the police to leave an anonymous tip. I waited until I saw the cops show up, and when they knocked on the door, my mom answered right away and seemed *very* confused. Not too long after, the police must have decided there wasn't anything to worry about and left. I hadn't seen the dog leave, so it must have hidden in the house somewhere.

I gotta find someplace to hide out for a bit. Maybe it will get bored and wander off. I shook the box and started to cut through my neighbor's lawn when I looked up and saw it. A tree-house. "That'll do just fine."

Scrambling up the ladder into the tree-house, I settled myself on the wooden floor and pulled out my computer. I looked to see what was still in the box. I took a quick inventory: a pair of clunky-looking glasses, a security camera, and a camcorder like Jimmy used for his vlogs.

Reaching down into the box, I pulled out the security camera and looked it over. Finding the USB port, I reached for the cable and plugged the camera into my laptop.

I saw that there was, in fact, a video on the older camera, and it was pretty good quality, too. I clicked the icon to play the video. The frame rate sucked, and it had no audio either, so I just watched as carefully as possible.

The video showed a place that looked like an old boiler room. It was either black and white or night vision, but either way, it was still quite dark. A single chair was placed in the center of the room, and an old wooden military footlocker was placed in front of it. I wasn't sure what it was, but something seemed very off about the video so far. Maybe it was the speed at which the light was flickering...

"Was this footage sped up?" I said aloud. From the timer's readout, it didn't seem like the footage was sped up, but instead, it was a time-lapse video.

The video itself must have been taken over several days to be as long as it was. But it didn't take long before something happened.

A man dressed in a familiar outfit started to walk into the shot. The way he walked through appeared to be in sync with the time-lapse. An unnerving smoothness, like you see in a

Claymation film, only with a person. As he wandered the room, I noticed a few things triggering me to remember my real father before he left my mom and me.

The strange man then sat in the chair behind the footlocker and waited with no movement. His face was obscured by the shadows of the room. But from the angle of his face, it was clear he was very focused on the old-wooden box. He sat quietly and absolutely still – so still that, until I saw him breathing, I thought the video had frozen.

It didn't take long for the creepy shit to start, though. It started slowly with the lid gently lifting as a slender hand grasped the edge. A high-heeled foot was what was pushing the lid open, as a slim-bodied woman twisted out of her strange contorted prison. Her body arched into a bridge-walking position, and with the same unusual sequencing with the camera's cycles, she moved around the room before settling behind the man.

She stood up with some unnatural balance and transitioned ever so smoothly as she draped her hand around the man's shoulders, almost as if she were a long-lost love. Her body was covered in a skin-tight leather outfit, and what appeared to be a cloth or leather gas mask was covering her face.

She began to dance and traveled all around the room with the skill and grace of a gymnast. Pulling at the tight outfit until it tore open. She then caressed the man's head, pulling it into the light, and I felt my stomach sink deep.

"Dad?"

She opened his mouth, sliding the strange fabric of her outfit in, and made him chew it up.

She resumed dancing, again and again, tearing off more of the suit and feeding it to my father.

I didn't know how to feel, other than scared out of my mind terrified. Knowing the type of video this was, I knew it wasn't going to end well. With each dance and subsequent hand feeding, my sense of dread only grew more intense. I felt tears in my eyes; she was now fully nude. But the graininess of the video compounded with the realization that I was potentially watching the death of my father.

I almost couldn't finish watching the video. "I need to know, though!"

That's when I looked back at the screen and saw the blood. She hadn't been pulling off her clothes but her... *Skin!*

"Jesus Christ, how are they even alive?" With each spin, more blood splattered the dingy walls like some sick modern art.

"Oh my God." As if she heard me, the woman stopped dancing, facing away from the camera. Her head tilted back, and her eyes seemed focused on mine. In that strange Claymation-like movement, she staggered over and looked directly into the lens – as if she was looking at *me* specifically.

"No way. There is no way this bitch is looking at me." Again, after finishing my sentence, her head tilted, and in the light, I could see her face.

She wasn't wearing a mask; her face WAS the mask. Her lips and lower jaw were distended and flapped in the wind like it was a flesh-covered gas mask filter. Her skin was pulled taut with some kind of steel wire corseting the back of her head, stretching the skin on her face smooth, and her eyes had small glass pieces embedded into her sockets to give the appearance of a gas mask.

As she looked at the camera and seemed to respond to what I was saying, her eyes started to track me. *What's going on here?*

Lifting her now blood-covered hand, she pulled the skin on her hands off like a glove and lifted one bloody finger to her trunk-like lips before turning to face my dad. I started to plead with the screen for her to not hurt him. I cried as she got closer and started giving him a lap dance smearing blood all over him as she danced in that jerky stop-go movement.

When the dance was done, she stood behind him, her eyes fixated on mine as her mouth stretched open, and she began sucking on his head like some sick blowjob. Each stroke revealed my father's face being shredded.

I was in shock. I tried to look away. I tried to stop the video, but the monstrous woman's eye contact had me frozen in fear. It was like she had a grip on my very soul. It was an agonizing ten minutes as with each stroke, she went deeper down on him. His upper body was now ripped apart to the bone in some places until finally, she swallowed him whole like a python.

Her body was engorged, but as she stood there, her chest and stomach started to constrict in sharp motions, shrinking her body back down to what it was originally.

Still not breaking eye contact, she danced seductively back to her footlocker and began dislocating her joints to fit back in and closed the lid.

Finally able to move again, I felt an unstoppable wave of emotion hit me as my father's disappearance now had an explanation. *He must have died in so much pain.* I sat there, head in my hands, crying, knowing that I couldn't do anything to save him.

He looked so old and disheveled, like he had been kept somewhere for a while before any of this happened.

I felt my phone vibrate, and I knew it was Jimmy, but I just didn't have the ability to deal with his bullshit tonight. I curled up and hugged my computer as I whimpered. "Goodbye, dad... I loved you."

Video: Friends

Waking up in the cold, damp morning light, I realized I was still in the treehouse. My laptop was almost dead, and the box of videos was still with me. I checked my phone after remembering that it had dinged with a message, and found one from Jimmy. "Hey bro, imma head over to da crazy bin for some more shots in the am, come join me. Maybe we will find some more of dem fucked up videos."

I dropped my phone, not wanting to think about that horrible place again. The thought of risking seeing that dog or the shadow-things again sent a shiver down my spine. But I also knew that Jimmy wasn't aware of what had happened.

Leaving my stuff and pocketing my phone, I ran to the old psych ward and prepared myself for the worst. I ran like my life depended on it. Even though I didn't like Jimmy that much, I didn't want him to die – or worse.

I finally reached the building after what felt like an eternity of running. My legs felt like noodles, and I dry-heaved from the stress on my stomach. As I straightened up, I felt like I was being crushed in a vise by the pressure of the darkness surrounding this building. The air was heavy with the evil that gave birth to those horrible videos. "I hope I'm not too late," I said aloud, just to hear the sound of my own voice. As I looked up at the windows, it seemed that the shadows inside were moving on their own, as if to get a better look at who was entering their domain.

Taking a deep breath, I walked up to the main door. It felt as if I was being physically pushed away from the building by the rising pressure. I grabbed the handles and forced my way in. It seemed like I was walking through some unseen liquid; my movements became more and more labored. "Jimmy!" I screamed to get his attention, or at least find out where he might be.

Looking up at the balconies overhead, I saw the shadows reaching down the walls, pointing in the direction of the old stairwell. I struggled forward through the dense air, but as I approached the door, the feeling of the slowing presence faded away.

Finally able to move without resistance, I stepped onto the landing. "Jimmy, where are you!" I shouted.

I finally heard a response. "Down here." His voice was faint but it sounded like he was okay.

Rounding the next landing, I stopped when I noticed that the door now stood agape. It was not just open, but mangled. The metal bar that had been welded in place now lay on the floor, torn free from its attachments.

"What the hell? What could have done this?" I stepped over the twisted pieces of metal and through the portal into the hallway. "Jimmy, you down here?"

After a few seconds, a clearer response came. "Yeah, over here, come check out dees cells!"

Looking at the sign next to the door, I saw that it was marked 'Enhanced Treatment.' "Oh, great," I muttered. "What psychos were housed here?" The echo of my words was muted by the padding that seemed to cover everything. I passed room after room, looking at the strange instruments and set-ups of equipment contained within. It was as if everyone just got up and left one day, leaving everything set up. Using the light on my phone, I scanned the area for any signs of Jimmy, but I couldn't even hear his annoying voice. "Hey, Jimmy! Where are you? This place isn't safe. We gotta get out of here!"

"I'm over here!" I heard his voice coming from down the hall in one of the rooms. "Just keep heading this way. I'm down here!"

Flashing my light down the hallway, I saw a shadow move into one of the rooms. *Oh, thank God, at least I know which room he's in now.* I jogged up to the door and rounded the corner into the room.

Everything went dark.

I WOKE UP IN A SMALL padded room. A putrid smell made me nauseous before I realized that I was laying next to a dead, incredibly rotted body next to me. A single illuminated light hung from the ceiling. A camera had been placed on the floor in the center of the light.

"Where am I... What happened?" I felt woozy, and my head was killing me.

Crawling over to the camera, I picked it up. I recognized it as the same camera that had been in the box. The words "Play Me" were scratched into the side of it.

Looking around, I saw a small window and the shadowed outline of a door. I ran over to it and started pounding on it, only for my screams to be muffled; my abuse of the door left unheard. "Let me out of here, you sick fuck! Why did you knock me out and put me in here?"

A piece of paper with the words "watch the video" scribbled on it filled the window, held there by an unseen hand.

"What? Are you freaking insane? Let me out of here, Jimmy, so I can kick your fucking ass!"

Another piece of paper appeared. "I'm not Jimmy."

I started to panic now. Some crazy person had me locked in a padded room in an abandoned asylum miles away from anywhere, and no one knew where I was. To make matters worse, what would happen to Jimmy when he arrived?

I didn't want to starve to death in this shitty place.

"If..." I started. "If I watch the video, will you let me out of here?"

About a minute passed when another sheet of paper appeared. "YES."

"Okay. I'll watch it."

My hands trembled as I opened the view screen. The camera automatically turned on, and I replayed the last video.

It started as the video Jimmy was shooting when we were on our way here. The day I found the box. He was doing his spiel and the video cut to a view of the inside of the asylum. I watched the video of the time after he and I split up. I noticed that, on a few occasions, he would stop, and the camera would whip around to try and catch some just out-of-sight blur. Out of nowhere, the dog jumped on top of him, knocking him to the ground. That attack was soon followed by me coming in from the doorway. After that, it went dark. *That's when it must have broken.*

When I left to explore the basement, the video skipped ahead. It now showed a video inside Jimmy's room. He was trying to fix something on his camera when he jumped from something hitting his window. His family lived in a first-floor apartment, so it wouldn't have been totally out of the question for an animal to try and get in at night.

He stood up and walked to the window, and I heard him laugh. "This little bitch ass dog, fucker followed me home." He proceeded to open the window and started whistling for the dog to come over.

"Wait a second. This isn't right. He told me about this."

"Come here, boy, come on," he whispered, and soon I saw the dog hop happily through the window and into his room. "Good boy," he said as he petted and scratched the dog's side.

"I guess he had a soft spot for the dog after all," I said aloud.

The video stopped again, and when it turned back on, the dog was walking away from the camera. It sat down beside the bed as Jimmy laid there asleep. The dog was dead still, like it was next to my mother. I started to fast forward the video.

The little dog sat there like that for about three hours before its head started to tilt back and its chest began to split open. Several small segmented tooth-like appendages uncurled from its fur, and a mouth opened wide. Its neck stretched up and tilted down before the camera's screen went glitchy and turned back on in a room with a single light source.

That's when it started to click. Looking away from the camera, I now noticed that the corpse in front of me wore the same clothing that Jimmy had on the night he was attacked by that creature.

"Jimmy?" I wanted to grab the body, roll it over to see if it was him, but I just didn't have the stomach for it.

I held the fast-forward button as I knew what was coming. It showed him stuck in this room over the last few days, screen going black every few minutes or so, probably to save battery or memory on the card. No food or water was ever brought to him. He started sitting and crying for long periods before eventually going insane, taking bites out of his arms but spitting them out, unable or not willing to swallow them. He tried time after time until finally succumbing to his wounds, passing out and dying there on the floor from blood loss or dehydration.

Stopping the video, I started to cry again. "First my dad and now this? What the fuck do you want from me? How is this possible? I just saw Jimmy the other day. Been texting him all week! How?"

Another piece of paper slid up the window. "Keep watching," it read.

I pressed play again, and after a few minutes of staring at my friend's lifeless body, the door to the room opened, and the dog from before trotted in. After lapping up some blood, it began to twist and contort its body, spasming on the ground as its body morphed into whatever it was changing into, which became clear very soon. When it finally settled, it had turned into a person.

Sitting up, its face came into the light, and I was dumbfounded how it had just transformed into Jimmy. It was indistinguishable. This thing was Jimmy now.

I heard the lock on the door pop, and the door slowly opened to a dark hallway. I heard footsteps coming from the shadows, and as the source of the sounds came into view, the light revealed the face of the dog, standing on its hind legs. Its eyes were strange – almost human – but with a deep reddish-brown color. It approached me, and I fell back in fear as its neck stretched and its face angled to look down at me.

I felt adrenaline rush into me, and I made a break for the door. Something heavy hit against my back, and I fell, landing on my friend's dead body with enough force that I heard his bones break. I felt a rib stab into me as it protruded out of my poor friend's chest. I screamed out in pain and rolled away as the creature whipped its head back down, crashing onto the exposed bone, impaling itself, and howling in pain. I staggered to my feet as it struggled to pull itself free. I stomped on its head to ensure it was stuck fast before running out the door, slamming it shut, and locking it closed.

I looked back at the window, and saw the enraged face of the dog as it slammed its head into the glass, cracking it but not breaking it. I felt the door budge while it tried to break it down, and I felt a wash of relief as it held firm. I turned and ran as fast and as far as I could. I was still fading in and out from whatever hit my head.

SOMEHOW, I MANAGED to end up on my doorstep. The last mile or two were a blur, but at least I was home, and that creature, whatever it was, was gone.

Opening the door, I saw my mom and Rob sitting at the table. It was surreal. There was a whole meal laid out. And Mom was laughing with Rob. "What... What's going on?"

"Oh, dear, you're home. Please join us for dinner."

Now I knew I needed to get to the hospital; I was clearly concussed. "What's going on?" I repeated.

They both turned to look at me like I was crazy. "What do you mean, hun? We were just having dinner. Please, come join the family." They both gestured to my seat, and I was incredibly tired. My body felt like a sack of potatoes, so I obeyed without questioning further.

My vision started to tunnel, and I fell back into my seat. My mother stood up, and I saw a glimpse of her eyes in the light. Her eyes were the same reddish-brown as that dog's eyes...

"It's okay, baby. You look exhausted. Take a nap. It will all be over soon, and we will be a happy family." When she finished speaking, her mouth opened, and her lower jaw popped and cracked as a camera lens came out. Rob stood up, and his body began splitting in half, with the same jointed teeth I'd seen in that cell. He reached towards me.

I tried to move, but my body was just too tired. Looking down, I noticed that I had been bleeding badly the whole time. I was simply too weak to run. Too weak to fight. The last thing I saw was my mother's neck stretching in order to get a higher vantage point to view whatever Rob was about to do to me. I felt my hands and feet go numb, and my vision narrowed into darkness...

www.ingramcontent.com/pod-product-compliance
Lightning Source LLC
Chambersburg PA
CBHW031448130726
47989CB00003B/1310